Socks for His Feet

TRISH DOTSON

Fulton Books, Inc.
Meadville, PA

Published by Fulton Books 2021

ISBN 978-1-63710-810-9 (paperback)
ISBN 978-1-63860-300-9 (hardcover)
ISBN 978-1-63710-811-6 (digital)

Printed in the United States of America

For Randi, Jake, Kate, and Ty.

I always tried my best to keep your feet warm.

The day he was born, she could not love him enough. When she looked into his innocent, helpless eyes, her heart melted. How could he ever know just how much she loved him?

What could she possibly do to show her love? She thought and thought. And as she thought, she brought his precious tiny soft bare feet to her lips. They were cold.

5

"Your little feet are so cold," she said to him.

He simply cooed at her.

She found the fluffiest pair of baby socks in his drawer, and she lovingly put them on his cold feet. He kicked his little legs and waved his little arms and cooed at her, and she was happy. Funny how putting socks on his feet made her feel love.

As he grew, he was always running around on his bare feet. She always asked him to put on his socks as he was running through the house. But he didn't want to.

8

When he was playing outside with his friends, she would yell out the window, "PUT ON YOUR SOCKS! YOUR FEET WILL GET COLD!" But he never did. He never understood why she always wanted him to wear his socks.

He didn't really like socks. They were never quite right. They were too baggy. They had too many bumps in the toes. They were too tight and made his toes not work quite right.

So she searched and searched and found the perfect pair. One that fit just right. No bumps or lumps. One where his toes felt right at home.

Whenever he had to wear socks, those were the ones—the perfect socks. When he wore them, it made her feel love.

He came home with his new uniform. Gold and blue jersey with the number 33 on the front and back. A helmet with a blue panther on the side. He made the team. With a smile on her face, she knew she had to find his perfect socks in the color gold.

She did.

He wore those socks for every game. He yelled from his room every Friday, "Mom! Where are my lucky socks?"

She watched every game from the stands. She knew on the cold, wet football field, his feet were warm, and she felt love.

After four years of football, his lucky socks were worn out. They were baggy, had holes in them, and needed to be thrown out.

But he kept them.

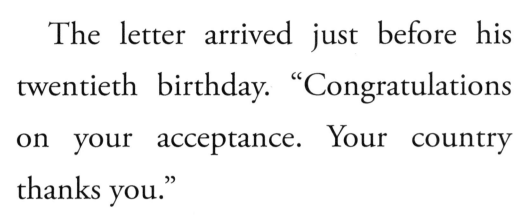

The letter arrived just before his twentieth birthday. "Congratulations on your acceptance. Your country thanks you."

As a tear slid down her face, she knew she would have to find his perfect socks in the color green.

She did.

When he packed his trunk to leave, with fear in her eyes, she handed him a supply of the perfect green socks. He hugged her goodbye and whispered in her ear, "Don't worry, Mom. I promise to wear my socks."

And she felt love.

He never saw it coming. The explosion was deafening.

As he lay in the hospital bed, he was missing his mother. He drifted off to sleep.

When she arrived at his bedside. She had his worn-out lucky socks.

As her baby lay sleeping, she pulled back the sheet and gently put the socks on his feet. She didn't know what else to do.

But when she put those old ragged socks on his feet, she felt love.

Now grown, with a baby of his own, he always made sure his son had warm socks on his feet. He wasn't sure why, but it made him feel love.

Years passed, and the call came. The time had come for him to say goodbye.

He rushed to her bedside. In his hand, his old ragged, holey, favorite pair of socks, the ones that always brought him luck.

As she lay in peaceful sleep, he pulled back the sheets and gently put those socks on her worn and weathered feet. And he felt love.

At that moment, he realized they weren't just socks. They weren't just to keep his feet warm and dry…

They were the emotions she couldn't contain.

They were the words impossible to speak.

They were the feelings that wouldn't fit inside her heart.

They were a symbol of her undying love.

As he looked at her, he finally understood.

He bent down and kissed her forehead and whispered in her ear, "Thank you, Mom, for always keeping my feet warm."

The End

About the Author

Trish was raised in a small town in Oklahoma. She has four children and five grandchildren. Trish wrote *Socks for His Feet* in 2012, where it sat on a shelf until 2018 when she lost her oldest son in a tragic car accident. She pulled it out again as a way of healing and a dedication to all her children. Trish is a screenwriter and author who lives with her husband of twenty-nine years, Colonel Robert Dotson, in Mesa, Arizona, where she continues to write and heal.

CPSIA information can be obtained
at www.ICGtesting.com
Printed in the USA
BVHW021430030821
613532BV00013B/526